W9-BLC-408

Werewolves

"Any book without a mistake in it has had too much money spent on it"

Sir William Collins, publisher

Werewolves

Nigel Suckling

ff&f

Werewolves

Published by
Facts, Figures & Fun, an imprint of
AAPPL Artists' and Photographers' Press Ltd.
10 Hillside, London SW19 4NH, UK
info@ffnf.co.uk www.ffnf.co.uk
info@aappl.com www.aappl.com

Sales and Distribution
UK and export: Turnaround Publisher Services Ltd.
orders@turnaround-uk.com
USA and Canada: Sterling Publishing Inc.
sales@sterlingpub.com
Australia & New Zealand: Peribo Pty.
peribomec@bigpond.com
South Africa: Trinity Books. trinity@iafrica.com

A catalogue record for this book is available
from the British Library.

ISBN 13: 9781904332466
ISBN 10: 1904332463

Design (contents and cover): Malcolm Couch
mal.couch@blueyonder.co.uk

Printed in China by Imago Publishing
info@imago.co.uk

Contents

Introduction

A garwolf is a savage beast
While the fury's on it at least
Eats men, wreaks evil, does no good
Living and roaming in the deep wood

Marie de France: *Bisclavret* 12th century

Traditionally, a werewolf or lycanthrope is someone who changes physically into something like a wolf, whether deliberately through magic, unconsciously through infection, or as the result of a curse. In this form they prowl the countryside attacking livestock and people – usually though not always women and children.

Some werewolves leave their bodies behind in a trance and just enter the minds of wild wolves.

The word werewolf literally means man-wolf in old Anglo-Saxon. Variations include garwolf, warwulf and warg, the term used by Tolkien in *The Hobbit* for the wolves that trap Bilbo and his friends up trees. In France and Haiti a werewolf is a *loup garou*.

In southern France, as in many other places, the full moon traditionally forces change upon a *loup garou*, whether they are willing or not. Often to make the change, werewolves dive into pools or fountains, from which they emerge hairy and wild. Later they dive into the same pool to change back.

The term lycanthropy – the condition of being a werewolf – comes from the Greek words *lycos* (wolf) and *anthropos* (man). Nowadays it is usually taken to mean the delusion of changing into a wolf, with accompanying savage ferocity.

In Greece werewolves and vampires are collectively known as *vrykolakas* and it is commonly believed throughout the Balkans that a werewolf will become a vampire after death.

In the Campania region of Italy it was traditionally believed that anyone born on Christmas night was liable the rest of their lives to become a werewolf for the Christmas period. In Sicily anyone born on the new moon is also likely to become a werewolf.

COMMON CAUSES OF BECOMING A WEREWOLF

Being bitten by a werewolf

Inheriting the condition from a parent

Being a seventh consecutive son or daughter

By choice and the use of magic potions or belts

Drinking water from a wolf's footprint

Drinking water downstream from a wolf

Eating the flesh (particularly the heart) of a wolf, or something it has killed (though in some places this is said to have the opposite effect of strengthening the eater against all kinds of devilry)

Eating human flesh, especially that of violent criminals

Being cursed by a sorcerer (or troll in Scandinavia)

Ways to Recognise a Werewolf

A werewolf may look like a natural wolf, but it will have human eyes

When in human form a werewolf will be pale, haggard and listless. He will tend to avoid direct sunlight and abhor cooked meat

After a spell of being in wolf form, the werewolf will be drained of energy and unable to leave bed for days

A werewolf cannot shed tears

In France they say that werewolf's hands are always broad and short-fingered, with hairy palms

Suspicious wounds identical to those reported as having been inflicted on a wolf nearby

Ways to Defend against Werewolves

Wear garlic

Wear a Greek or Turkish Lucky Eye charm

Wear a silver cross

Have silver bullets in your gun

Carry a consecrated host, communion wine or holy water

Avoid dark woods at night, especially under the full moon

A werewolf can be cured by being cut or struck in the forehead so that blood flows freely; or by having three drops of blood drawn with a needle

A werewolf can also be cured by love, which dampens its wilder urges. Or by calling its true name three times

WAYS TO DESTROY A WEREWOLF

Chop off a limb and it will regain its human form

Shoot it with silver bullets or arrows, or stab it with a silver knife

Pierce it through the heart with a wooden (preferably aspen or whitethorn) stake
The only sure way to destroy a werewolf and prevent either its revival or its becoming a vampire is to cremate its head, heart or complete body. A dying werewolf regains its human form

Across Europe it was once widely believed that if a wolf saw a person first, they would be struck dumb. As the poet Dryden put it "*My Voice grows hoarse; I feel the Notes decay / As if the Wolves had seen me first today.*"

In Scandinavian tradition a sorcerer can become a werewolf either by actually changing shape into a wolf, or by leaving his human body behind in a trance and entering into a spectral or actual wild wolf.

Canon Pierre Mamor of Saintes in his *Flagellum Maleficorum* (*Scourge of the Witches*) 1490 reached the conclusion that werewolves were real wolves possessed by demons or sorcerers, but also told the tale he had heard of a wife in Lorraine whose husband had vomited up a child's hand. He had then confessed to having eaten the child while in wolf form.

Some people choose to become werewolves by magical means such as the rubbing on of ointment, whose ingredients may include potent narcotics like belladonna (Deadly Nightshade), aconite (Wolf Bane), opium and henbane. Alternatively one can use a wolf-belt – a charmed belt that changes the nature of its wearer. This is probably a remnant of the more ancient shamanic practice of wearing a complete wolf-pelt.

The potion used by werewolves to transform is similar to that used by witches and wizards to become cats, owls, hares, foxes and many other creatures, including of course wolves.

The doctor and philosopher Giambattista della Porta (1535 – 1615) recorded that in Naples in his day the country folk often nailed the heads of wolves over their doors to guard against sorcerers and witches.

Recipes for transforming potions that survive from the sixteenth century in Giambattista della Porta's *Natural Magick* (Book Eight) suggest infusing mandrake, stramonium or solanum manicum, belladonna or henbane in a cup of wine. Usually one at a time, though some recipes contain a cocktail of these and other potent herbs.

One flying ointment recipe suggests adding to skimmed animal fat hemlock, aconite, poplar leaves and soot. Another suggests cowbane (*sium*), cinquefoil (*pentaphyllon*), bat's blood and Deadly Nightshade. These ointments were rubbed into the skin, usually in sensitive areas like the groin.

The belt which some werewolves claimed as their means of transformation was either wolf-hide or human skin taken from an executed criminal. Its girth was three fingers. Stubbe Peeter, executed in Bedburg for being a werewolf in 1589, claimed to have had such a belt given him by his personal demon. He would tie it on whenever the urge to rampage came upon him.

Henri Boguet (1550 – 1619), the dreaded Witchfinder of Burgundy, claimed many confessions from lycanthropes in which "To turn themselves into wolves, they first rubbed themselves with an ointment, and then Satan clothed them in a wolf's skin which completely covered them, and that they then went on all-fours and ran about the country chasing now a person and now an animal according to the guidance of their appetites."

Boguet also dealt with the case of Perrenette Gandillon. The story went that a boy called Benoist Bidel had been out collecting fruit with his little sister. On one occasion when he climbed a tree and she stood waiting below, she was suddenly attacked by a wolf. Benoist jumped down to defend his sister and managed to hold the wolf at bay till help came and it was severely beaten into retreat.

The boy died of his wounds, but not before saying that the wolf had seemed to have human hands. At the same time a woman in the village died of mysterious injuries identical to those inflicted on the wolf, and the villagers realised that she must have been it.

Belief in werewolves is found wherever there are populations of wild wolves. The werewolf of popular fiction draws mainly on old European traditions fostered during the long age of hostility towards, and superstition about, wolves. In England belief in werewolves died out in the fifteenth or sixteenth centuries after the eradication of wild wolves. In France, Germany and other European countries it persisted much longer.

In Perigord in France it was believed into the nineteenth century that at the full moon some local youths, particularly the sons of priests, were compelled to go into the woods to a certain pool where they would dive in naked.

When they emerged they would find wolf pelts left by a demon, which they put on and roamed the night as wolves. To change back they removed the hide, dived into the pool again and would emerge as themselves.

Wolves generally avoid humans but in harsh weather they have always preyed on them and their livestock. In 1875 it was estimated that 161 people in Russia were killed by wolves.

In Anglo Saxon Britain January was called Wolf Month because it held the greatest danger of being attacked by starving wolves.

Egbert, Archbishop of York, who died in 766, decreed that animals which had been attacked by wolves should be killed and not eaten as a precaution against people becoming werewolves.

King Edgar of England (952 - 975) is often credited with having rid the country of wolves by commuting an annual tribute of gold and luxuries from Ludwall (Idwall), King of Wales, into 300 wolf pelts. Within four years scarcely a wolf remained, though it is unlikely the eradication was really complete till some centuries later. It just felt that way, relatively speaking, because wolves ceased to be a serious factor in most English and Welsh lives.

Thrice famous Saxon King, on whom time ne'er shall prey,
O Edgar! Who compeldst our Ludwall hence to pay
Three hundred Wolves a yeere for trybute unto thee:
And for that trybute payd, as famous may'st thou be,
O conquer'd British King, by whome was first destroy'd
The multitude of Wolves, that long this land annoy'd.

Michael Drayton *Polybion* 1612

In the *Annales Cambriae* it was recorded that in 1166 a mad wolf attacked twenty-two people, all of whom shortly died, probably from rabies.

In the fourteenth century the village of Wormhill in Derbyshire was still held on an annual tribute of wolf heads. There is a strong local tradition that the last wolf in

England was killed at Wormhill Hall in the fifteenth century.

The last wolf in Scotland is believed to have been killed in 1743 at a remote spot near Pall-a-chrocain in the Tarnaway Forest in Moray, near the mouth of the Findhorn River. The story goes that after a 'black beast' had killed a mother and two children, the local Laird Mackintosh had called in a famous hunter called MacQueen.

A day and place were fixed for the hunt to begin and when it came the laird and his party waited in vain for MacQueen to appear. Finally he arrived when the morning was almost done. Seeing the impatience on their faces the hunter asked innocently. "What's your hurry?" And then from his bag he tipped out the wolf's bloody head.

The laird was so impressed he gave MacQueen the land known as Sean-achan.

Ireland in the seventeenth century was often nicknamed Wolf Land because of its abundance of the creatures. Irish Wolf Hounds were bred specially to defend against them but even so they took longer to be exterminated than in the rest of the British Isles. The last reliable sighting of a wolf in Ireland was in 1786 when one was hunted down and killed near Mt Leinster in County Carlow for attacking sheep. There are later claims but none backed by solid evidence.

In Germany wild wolves finally died out at the beginning of the nineteenth century, but returned in 1998, swimming across the river Neisse from Poland and breeding in the Spree valley.

In Denmark there is a tradition that if a woman takes the placenta left by a new born foal, stretches it out between four sticks and then crawls naked through it she will give birth painlessly – but her sons will be werewolves and her daughters witches.

In many parts of Europe it was once believed that babies born with a caul (placenta) over their heads were liable to become werewolves.

CHAPTER I:

Primal Scream: Myths and Legends

The earliest mention of a werewolf is in the Epic of Gilgamesh c.2000 BC where, in tablet six, the goddess Ishtar is described as changing a shepherd into a wolf. Gilgamesh's wild companion Enkidu is also seen by some as a prototype werewolf.

In the sixth century BC the Babylonian king Nebuchadnezzar was seized with a lycanthropic-type madness that caused him to run off into the wild where "his heart was made like the beasts" and he "did eat grass as oxen, and his body was wet with the dew of heaven, till his hairs were grown like eagles' feathers, and his nails like birds' claws" (Daniel I chs 4, 5).

Herodotus, writing in the fifth century BC mentions in *Melpomene* a tribe called the Neuri living north-east of Scythia by the Baltic Sea who, according to the Scythians, were sorcerers who changed themselves into wolves for a few days each year (*Histories* iv; 105).

MARCELLUS SIDETES, a famous physician in the reign of Antoninus Pius (AD 138-161) wrote of werewolves: "*Men afflicted with the disease of so-called cynanthropy or lycanthropy go out by night in the month of February in imitation of wolves or dogs in all respects, and they tend to hang around tombs until daybreak.*

"*These are the symptoms that will allow you to recognize the sufferers from this disease. They are pallid, their gaze is listless, their eyes are dry, and they cannot produce tears. You will observe that their eyes are sunken and their tongue is dry, and they are completely unable to put on weight. They feel thirsty, and their shins are covered in lacerations which cannot heal because they are continually falling down and being bitten by dogs. Such are their symptoms.*

"*One must recognize that lycanthropy is a form of melancholia. You will treat it by opening a vein at the time of its manifestation and draining the blood until the point of fainting. Then feed the patient with food conducive to good humours. He is to be given sweet baths. After that, using the whey of the milk, cleanse him over three days with the gourd-medicine of Rufus or Archigenes or Justus. Repeat this a second and third time after intervals.*

"*After the purifications one should use the antidote to viper bites. Take the other measures too prescribed earlier for melancholia. As evening arrives and the disease manifests itself apply to the head the lotions that usually induce sleep and anoint the nostrils with scents of this sort and opium. Occasionally supply sleep-inducing drinks also.*"

In the *Satyricon* Petronius (c.27-66 AD) describes a soldier turning into a werewolf who then ravaged a herd of cattle. In wolf form he was seriously wounded and later the soldier was found to have identical injuries.

In ancient Egypt Wepwawet was the wolf-headed god of war whose cult centre was at Atef-Khent (called Lycopolis by the Greeks) in Upper Egypt. He was later absorbed into the figure of Anubis, the jackal-headed guide of the dead into the underworld.

One of the earliest lycanthropes on record comes in the ancient Greek legend of Lycaon, the first king of Arcadia. The story goes like this: A time came when Zeus (or Jupiter) grew alarmed at the clamour of misery rising from Earth and decided to pay a visit to see what was going on for himself.

He visited Arcadia where there were rumours of cannibalism and human sacrifice. Although travelling in human guise, Zeus sent omens ahead warning Lycaon through his priests that a god was coming. The king decided to put this to the test. Deciding that only a god would be able to tell, he had a visiting ambassador killed and butchered and cooked into succulent dishes for a feast. When Zeus came knocking, he was invited in to the feast with a show of hospitality and in due course presented with the dish of human flesh. In fury Zeus overturned the table and set fire to the palace. Lycaon fled into the countryside but as he ran a hideous change came over him.

Here is how Zeus described it later to the other gods on Mt Olympus:

> *"The tyrant in terror, for shelter gains*
> *Neighbouring fields and scours along the plains.*
> *Howling he fled, and he fain would have spoke*
> *But human voice his brutal tongue forsook.*
> *About his lips the gathered foam he churns,*
> *And, breathing slaughters, still with rage he burns,*
> *But on the bleating flock his fury turns.*
> *His mantle, now his hide, with rugged hairs*
> *Cleaves to his back; a famished face he bears;*
> *His arms descend, his shoulders sink away*
> *To multiply his legs for chase of prey.*
> *He grows a wolf, his hoariness remains,*
> *And the same rage in other members reigns.*
> *His eyes still sparkle in narrower space:*
> *His jaws keep the grin and violence of his face."*

Ovid: *Metamorphoses* Bk1

By the way, not content with turning Lycaon into a wolf, this incident decided Zeus that it was time to start the world again. So he released a great flood that destroyed all humanity save Deucalion and Pyrrha, from whom the human race was reborn after their boat finally landed on Mt Parnassus.

These herbs of bane to me did Moeris give,
In Pontus culled, where baneful herbs abound.
With these full oft have I seen Moeris change
To a wolf's form, and hide him in the woods.

Virgil's eighth *Eclogue* (first century BC)

Pliny the Elder (first century AD) tells in his famous *Natural History* that a man of the Anteus clan (Lycaon's descendants) was periodically selected by lot and taken to a lake in Arcadia where he hung his clothes on an ash tree and swam across. This changed him into a wolf and he was condemned to wander in this form for nine years. If he attacked no humans in that time he could swim back and was changed back into human shape.

According to Pausanias (Greek traveller, second century AD), an Arcadian named Damarchus won a gold medal for boxing at the Olympic Games in 400 BC after spending nine years as a werewolf. Pausanias also records the tradition of the Anteus clan producing werewolves and hints that they still practised human sacrifice on Mt Lycaeus while he was visiting.

The ancient Roman festival of Lupercalia (15 February) was probably named after the she-wolf that suckled Romulus and Remus after they were set adrift on the Tiber, as the festivities centred on the cave where this was said to have taken place. After sacrificing a goat and a dog two young men made whips of their hide and then ran naked around the city ceremonially flogging anyone they met to drive out evil spirits and encourage fertility. There was also much attendant drunkenness and debauchery.

When Christianity became Rome's official religion, the Church did its best to discourage Lupercalia but it was so popular that it was not until 496 AD that the Pope finally banned the event as a pagan aberration and replaced it with the feast of St Valentine.

ST CHRISTOPHER, the patron saint of travellers (famous for carrying the child Jesus across a river, only to feel he was carrying the weight of the whole world) is almost as famous among eastern Orthodox Christians as he is in the west; but in the east they tell a slightly different tale.

FOR A START, in Orthodox religious art St Christopher is traditionally shown as having a dog's head (cynocephalic). The eastern legend goes that around the year 300 AD a soldier named Reprobus was captured by the Romans in battle with the Marmaritac, a Berber tribe from Cyrene, west of Egypt. This was supposedly a dog-headed tribe of cannibals, and apart from this Reprobus is also said to have been a giant.

However, despite this unpromising background, Reprobus was drafted into the Roman army. He also converted to Christianity under the name Christopher (bearer of Christ) and, after being shipped to Antioch in Syria with many of his tribe, began converting others to Christianity – so many in fact that he was sentenced to death by the persecuting Antioch governor (or some say the Roman Emperor himself). Despite miraculously surviving several attempts at martyrdom the legend says he finally died and his body was taken back to his homeland by Bishop Peter of Alexandria, where he was revered under the name St Menas.

One likely explanation for the eastern St Christopher's monstrous appearance is that 'dog-headed cannibals' was a Greco-Roman term of casual abuse for people living beyond the bounds of the empire, especially in Africa. It was probably used as such in the earliest Greek accounts of the saint and then taken literally by later scribes.

The existence of dog-headed people was taken for granted by Giambattista della Porta (1535-1615) who in his *Natural Magick* 1584 (Bk 1; Ch 8) confidently gives this bit of advice on keeping track of the progress of the moon: "*The beast Cynocephalus rejoices at the rising of the Moon, for then he stands up, lifting his fore-feet toward Heaven, and wears a Royal Ensign upon his head. And he has such a sympathy with the Moon, that when she meets with the Sun (as between the old and new Moon) so that she gives no light, the male, or he-Cynocephalus, never looks up, nor eats anything, as bewailing the loss of the Moon; and the female, as malcontent as he, all that while pisses blood. For which causes, these beasts are nourished and kept in hallowed places, that by them the time of the Moon's meeting with the Sun may be certainly known.*"

In Ethiopia it was once believed that most, if not all, blacksmiths could turn into hyenas, in which shape they prowled graveyards looking for flesh to eat. For which reason no visitors would accept meat in a blacksmith's house unless they had seen it killed with their own eyes. Blacksmiths also wore gold earrings and many hunters claimed to have killed hyenas with gold rings in their ears.

St Christopher is not the only dog-headed saint though the next one demands less credulity. In the thirteenth century Etienne de Bourbon, an Inquisitor travelling France in search of heresy, wrote: "*This recently happened in the diocese of Lyons where . . . numerous women confessed that they had taken their children to Saint Guinefort. As I thought that this was some holy person, I continued with my enquiry and finally learned that this was actually a greyhound, which had been killed in the following manner.*"

The story was that a local lord had left his trusted hound Guinefort to guard his baby while it slept. When a commotion was heard and he came to check, he saw blood all over the crib and around the dog's mouth. Drawing the obvious conclusion, he seized his bow and shot the beast dead. Then the baby started crying and turned out to be completely unharmed, and under the crib was found a dead snake . . .

In his grief and repentance the lord buried the hound in a well, planting a grove of trees around it which became a place of pilgrimage. Well, the Inquisition was having none of this of course and had the shrine dismantled, but the legend of the faithful martyred hound lived on.

In some parts of Greece it is (or used to be) believed that even eating the flesh of a sheep killed by a common wolf could turn a person into a werewolf.

Also in Greece a child born between Christmas and the Twelfth Night (Jan 5) is likely to become a *callicantzaros*, closely related to the werewolf, after death – appearing between Christmas and Twelfth Night each year to tear people to pieces with its extended, claw-like fingernails. The rest of the year it exists in some netherworld. To prevent a 'feast-blasted' child turning into one of these half-human, half-animal monsters, it was held over a fire by its parents until its feet were scorched.

In Greece and neighbouring countries it is also believed possible to be turned into a werewolf through a curse – the Lycaeonia curse. This and other curses can be warded off by wearing a lucky eye as jewellery. These are usually blue and are common in any Greek or Turkish market. Alternatively, wear or carry garlic.

In many Balkan countries being born on Christmas Day is likely to turn one into a werewolf, for boys at least. Girls become witches.

In Italy it is believed that anyone who sleeps outdoors on a Friday night with a full moon will either be attacked or turned into a werewolf. Many drunkards are said to have become werewolves this way.

In Estonia it is believed possible to become a werewolf by accident or by being cursed. The spell can be broken by having someone recognise and call you by your Christian name, so Estonian werewolves tend to stalk their nearest and dearest hoping for recognition and rarely doing them any direct harm.

In parts of Estonia and Latvia the Brothers Grimm found a legend of a limping boy who goes around the villages after Christmas calling all those who have succumbed to the devil in the past year. If they refuse, his gigantic companion rounds them up with a whip of chains and drives them along. As they follow the boy, the sinners change into wolves and in this form they savage any cattle or sheep they can find, though they cannot hurt humans. Then after twelve days the spell is broken and they return home in human form, though often with scars from their whipping.

Bishop Olaus Magnus (1490 – 1558), renowned chronicler of strange customs and beliefs in the sixteenth century (most famously sea monsters), gave his opinion that werewolves were far more destructive than 'true and natural' wolves. He also described a similar tradition of Christmas werewolves in the Baltic region: "*On the feast of the Nativity of Christ, at night, such a multitude of wolves transformed from men gather together in a certain spot arranged among themselves, and then spread to rage with wondrous ferocity against human beings and those animals which are not wild, that the natives of these regions suffer more detriment from these, than they do from true and natural wolves; for when a human habitation has been detected by them isolated in the woods, they besiege it with atrocity, striving to break in the doors, and in the event of their doing so, they devour all the human beings, and every animal which is found within.*"

Olaus Magnus also reports: *"The wife of a nobleman in Livonia* (Baltic coast) *expressed her doubts to one of her slaves whether it were possible for man or woman thus to change shape. The servant at once volunteered to give her evidence of the possibility. He left the room, and in another moment a wolf was observed running over the country. The dogs followed him, and notwithstanding his resistance, tore out one of his eyes. Next day the slave appeared before his mistress blind of an eye."*

Near the small town of Mazsalaca in northern Latvia, a mile or two downriver, is a tree known as the Werewolf Pine where wizards are supposed to change into werewolves by crawling among the roots under a full moon muttering certain incantations.

On Lycanthropy

> *This malady, saith Avicenna, troubleth men most in February, and is nowadays frequent in Bohemia and Hungary, according to Huerniua. Schernitzius will have it common in Livonia.*
>
> Robert Burton *Anatomy of Melancholy* 1621

The principality of Polotsk in what is now Belarus was ruled for the second half of the eleventh century by a reputed werewolf. In legends which spread even during his lifetime, Prince Vseslav Bryacheslavovich, or Vseslav Chorodney (the Magician), was rumoured to have been conceived by magic and born with a large and vivid birthmark on his head that he usually hid with a headband.

Because of his magical conception Vseslav was believed able to transform himself into a wolf, a falcon or a deer with golden horns. Although occasionally fierce in battle, establishing his land as a major force in the region to rival Kiev in neighbouring Ukraine, he seems not to have suffered the usual rages of werewolves and is remembered as a great hero in Belarus history. He also imported Byzantine architects to build a great cathedral in honour of St Sofia.

In Russia werewolves or *volkodlaki* may be recognized by the bristles remaining under their tongues while in human guise. Both werewolves and vampires can be destroyed by being pierced through the heart with an aspen stake.

In Armenia it is believed that great sins can be enough to turn some women into werewolves. A spirit appears and forces them to put on a wolf skin whereupon they devour their own children, then those of relatives and friends, then any children they can find. This lasts for seven years unless they are first killed. By night they prowl as wolves but by day they can remove the wolf skin and seem almost normal.

OLD RUSSIAN SPELL FOR BECOMING A WEREWOLF

If you wish to become a werewolf, seek in the forest a hewn down tree. Stab it with a small copper knife and walk around the tree reciting this incantation:

In the wide sweeping ocean, on the island Bujan
On the open plain the Moon shines on an aspen stump
Into the green wood, into the gloomy vale.
Towards the herd creeps a shaggy wolf
His fangs sharpened for the horned cattle
But into the wood the wolf does not go
He dives not into the shadowy vale
Moon, moon! Golden horned moon!
Melt the bullet; blunt the hunter's knife
Splinter the shepherd's staff
Cast terror upon all cattle
Upon men and all creeping things
That they may not seize the grey wolf
That they may not rend his warm hide!
My word is binding, firmer than sleep
More binding than the promise of heroes!

Then jump over the tree three times and you will be changed and run off into the trees as a wolf.

In Germany it used to be said that a horse which survives being bitten by a wolf will gallop much faster than before.

In Malory's *Morte d'Arthur* (Bk XIX ch 11) one of the knights of the Round Table, Sir Marrock, is said to have been betrayed by his wife who had turned him into a werewolf for seven years.

Around the year 450 AD Saint Patrick of Ireland is said to have transformed Vereticus, a Welsh king, into a wolf.

In Norse saga Ingiald, the son of King Aunund was very timid as a child but grew up to be the boldest of warriors after eating the heart of a wolf.

In the Icelandic *Volsungsaga* the hero Sigmund's father and brothers are killed off by a shape-shifting witch in the form of a wolf. Later Sigmund and his son become werewolves themselves by wearing enchanted wolf-skins.

Later in the same saga, after Sigmund has shaken off his lycanthropy, Sigmund is trapped along with nine companions in some stocks by their enemies. Each night a she-werewolf comes and eats one of them until only Sigmund is left. His sister comes to his rescue. She is unable to free him but has a servant fill his mouth with honey. When the werewolf comes, she smells the honey

IN NORSE MYTHOLOGY Loki, god of mischief, fathered three monsters on the giantess Angrboda. One was the Midgard Serpent, another was Hel (which means Death) and the third was Fenris the wolf.

When the other gods learned of this they remembered prophecies of the disaster these creatures would bring into the world. So Odin the Allfather cast the Midgard Serpent into the depths of the ocean where she grew so large she finally encompassed the whole world with her tail in her mouth. Hel was given charge of Nifhelm, the underworld to which go all those who suffer the humiliation of not dying in battle.

Fenris they tried to tame but soon only Tyr, god of war, was brave enough to handle the growing wolf monster. They tried chaining him but Fenris just snapped their strongest chains like straw. So the gods asked the dwarves to make them an unbreakable chain, which they did, from the footstep of a cat, the roots of a mountain, a woman's beard, the breath of fishes, the sinews of a bear, and a bird's spittle. What's more, this unbreakable chain looked no more substantial than a ribbon.

The problem was how to persuade Fenris to let them bind him, because he was now so big that even Tyr was afraid to go near. So they used a trick and asked Fenris to test the magic chain for them to see if it really was as strong as the dwarves claimed. Fenris agreed, but only if Tyr would let him hold one hand in his jaws. This was done and when the wolf failed to break free, Tyr paid with the price of his hand for the victory. In triumph the gods chained Fenris to a rock a mile deep in the earth where he is destined to remain till the great battle at the end of time.

and begins to lick Sigmund's mouth. Immediately he bites her tongue and pulls it right out of her head by the roots so that she dies.

Norse *berserkers* were warriors who went into battle wearing wolf or bear skins after having worked themselves up into a furious state (with or without herbal assistance) in which they became totally fearless, indifferent to pain, howled like beasts and were prone to bite through the iron rims of their shields in their impatience to get into battle. After the fit passed though, they became as weak as babies for a while.

Berserkers were often feared as much by their own countrymen as by their enemies as they were liable to pick fights for the flimsiest of reasons, or just plain boredom. Under Norwegian law, any farmer who refused a challenge to arms forfeited his land and family and many *berserkers* grew rich this way.

In the *Vatnsdaela Saga* Thorir is an unwilling *berserker* because he has no control over his fits. However, his brother Thorsteinn knows of a solution. They rescue a baby that happens to have been exposed to the elements to die. Thorir takes it home and rears it as his own son as a sacrifice to the Creator, and the fits never trouble him again.

Viking marauders were often called simply 'wolves' in medieval chronicles, leading to later confusion and their massacres being attributed either to werewolves or real ones. This contributed greatly to the demonisation of real wolves in Europe.

Vargr in Norse means wolf, godless person or outlaw.

IN NORWAY it was once believed possible for sorcerers, werewolves and malicious fairies to put a curse of lycanthropy on anyone who came their way without taking proper precautions, such as wearing garlic or a silver cross or even just having said their daily prayers.

An illustration is the talc of Lasse, a cottager in a tiny village in the forest. One day he went off into the woods as usual but failed to return. Days, weeks and then months went by with no sign of him, till his wife was sure he must have died in some accident.

Years went by till one Christmas Eve a beggar woman came to the kitchen door. The good wife took her in, treated her kindly and fed her well. As she was leaving, the beggar woman said, "Your husband is not dead you know. These past

Palgrave's *Rise and Progress of the English Commonwealth* (1832) states confidently that among the Anglo Saxons an outlaw was said to have the head of a wolf.

In Denmark there was once a man who was a werewolf from childhood but grew up without anyone, even his wife, suspecting. Then one evening returning from a fair with his wife in a cart, he felt the change coming over him. Giving the reins to his wife, he told her that if anything attacked, she had only to strike at it with her apron to be safe. Then he ran into the trees and soon

few years he has been condemned to roam the forest as a wolf, always afraid the hunters will get him."

That evening as she was putting meat in the pantry for the next day, the good wife turned to find a wolf staring at her from the pantry steps with a pleading look in its eyes.

"If only I were sure you are my Lasse, I would give you this meat," she said. And at that moment the wolf-skin fell away and she beheld her husband as she had last seen him.

Which goes to show again that, in Scandinavia at least, love alone can quench the fiery passions of the werewolf.

Sabine Baring-Gold
The Book of Werewolves 1865

afterwards she was attacked by a great ravening wolf.

Hopelessly she flapped at it with her apron, from which it wrenched a piece and then to her astonishment ran away. Shortly afterwards her husband returned with the cloth still in his mouth and confessed to being a werewolf, but said that she had cured him. And indeed he was never troubled by the fits from that day. Perhaps the apron reminded him in his animal fury of the other, gentler side of his life.

When Sweden was overrun with wolves during its war with the Russians in the early nineteenth century, many Swedes believed that the Russians were turning their prisoners into wolves and sending them back to plague their homeland.

In the Netherlands a young man was once on his way to an archery contest in Rousse when he saw a large wolf attacking a maid who was tending cows at pasture. Raising his bow, he shot the wolf in its flank and it ran off with the arrow stuck deep. Later the young man heard that one of the Burgomaster's servants lay wounded by an arrow, and when he visited the servant he recognised his own arrow. On his deathbed the servant confessed to having eaten children as a werewolf.

In Poland they say that if a witch lays a girdle of human skin across the threshold of a house where a wedding is being celebrated, the bride and groom will be changed to werewolves if they step over it. Only after three years can the witch reverse the spell if she wishes.

AROUND 1285 Gerald of Wales, while visiting Ireland, was told the strange tale of a priest who had encountered a werewolf couple in County Meath two years earlier. One night while sitting by a campfire beneath a leafy tree with only a boy for company, the priest was alarmed by the approach of a large wolf.

"Don't be afraid!" said the wolf quite clearly. "You have nothing to fear."

This speech in some ways was just as alarming as the beast's appearance, but after a while of questioning the priest calmed down enough to hear its tale:

"We are natives of Ossory," the speaking wolf began. "Because of the curse of a local saint, the abbot Natalis, two people – a man and a woman – are forced every seven years into exile not only from their home, but also from their bodily form. They put off their human shape and take that of a wolf. If they survive the seven years, two others take their place the same way, and the first pair return to their former home and nature."

Unfortunately, he continued, his female partner was dying and wanted the priest to administer the last rites. With fear and misgivings, the priest allowed himself to be led to the dying she-wolf, who could also speak and who resumed human form during the administration of the sacrament. The next morning the man-wolf set the priest and his boy back on their way, promising to repay the kindness if ever possible

Gerald was unable to test the truth of the matter but, along with several local bishops, was convinced of the priest's sincerity and an official record of the marvel was sent to Rome, as well as being recorded in Gerald's own famous *Topography of Ireland* (Part 2).

In Portugal werewolves were once believed very common and called *lobis-homems*. They were especially widespread in the fifteenth century, but they were mostly considered harmless because they were terrified of light and the slightest spark or lantern gleam would drive them away into the shadows.

Ossory in Ireland was long considered a haven of werewolves. One of many old chronicles to mention this was the *Fitness of Names* which says the founder of an Ossory clan was named: "Laignech *Faelad*, that is, he was the man that used to shift into *faelad*, i.e. wolf-shapes. He and his offspring after him used to go whenever they pleased into the shapes of the wolves and, after the custom of wolves, kill the herds."

CHAPTER II

Howling at the Moon: Werewolves in History

When Bad King John of England died in 1216 he was rumoured to have become a werewolf. The story goes that after he sickened and suddenly died at Swineshead Abbey near Bolton, Lancs (rumoured to have been poisoned by a monk), he was buried in Worcester Cathedral between its patron saints Oswald and Wulfstan. Soon noises were heard from his grave – howls and shrieks and thumping. The Canons of the Cathedral disinterred the body and disposed of it on some unconsecrated waste ground nearby that was afterwards haunted by a half-man half-wolf.

In the thirteenth century it became considered heretical by the Church to deny the existence of werewolves although centuries previously St Augustine and Thomas Aquinas had decided lycanthropy was a mad delusion, however convincing to both sufferer and victims.

However, it was also heretical to believe that Satan was able to produce werewolves from his own power against the will of God because only God could create new life, the Devil could only distort or twist whatever had already been created.

Trial records show that between 1520 and 1630 an estimated 30,000 people in France were accused of lycanthropy and/or witchcraft, many pleading guilty under torture and suffering painful execution, usually by fire which was believed to purge the sinners' souls and offer them a chance of redemption.

In 1631 the famous witch trial judge Pierre de Lancre died, proudly claiming to have overseen the torture and burning of over 600 suspects.

The werwolves are certayne sorcerers, who having annoynted their bodies with an oyntment which they make by the instinct of the devil, and putting on a certayne inchaunted girdle, doe not onely unto the view of others seeme as wolves, but to their owne thinking have both the shape and nature of wolves, so long as they weare the said girdle. And they do dispose themselves as very wolves, in wourrying and killing, and most of humane creatures.

Richard Verstegan
Restitution of Decayed Intelligence, 1628

Fifty years after the case of Burgot and Verdun there was another panic in the same area caused by the disappear-

ONE FAMOUS WEREWOLF case in France is that of two peasants, Pierre Burgot and Michel Verdun, tried in 1521 by judge Jean Bodin (or Boin), prior of the Dominican Priory in Poligny near the French border with Switzerland. Under interrogation Burgot 'confessed' that nineteen years earlier, while trying to herd his flock of sheep during a violent storm, he was approached by three dark and mysterious horsemen. Their leader promised safety for his sheep both then and in future, plus gold, if only Burgot would submit to him as lord.

Well, there seemed nothing to lose so Burgot submitted and not only received gold but his flock survived the storm and thrived greatly afterwards. But the next time he met his mysterious benefactor, his new lord demanded that he renounce his Christian faith because he was of course an emissary of Satan himself called Moyset.

Burgot had little choice in the moment but to submit again, though he greatly regretted his pact and would have unmade it if possible (or so he confessed). Then one day he was approached by Michel Verdun, another of Satan's servants, who forced him to rub magic ointment on his body, whereupon he changed into a wolf. Then as were-wolves Burgot and Verdun ravaged the countryside and among the crimes for which they were convicted were the killing of a woman, the tearing apart of a seven-year-old boy and the abduction of a four-year-old girl, whom they devoured completely as she was so delicious.

After being executed by fire at Besançon, a picture of these werewolves was hung in the local church as a warning to any others tempted to make pacts with the devil.

ance and later discovery, half-eaten, of several children. A reward was posted by the town authorities of Dole and two months later Gilles Garnier, nicknamed The Hermit of Dole, was arrested, caught in the act of eating a freshly killed boy of twelve. His trial and execution by fire were long celebrated in folk song.

There are two kinds of werewolves, voluntary and involuntary. The voluntary were, of course, wizards, such as Gilles Garnier, who on 18 January, 1573, was condemned by the court of Dôle, Lyons, to be burned alive for "the abominable crimes of lycanthropy and witchcraft." More than fifty witnesses deposed that he had attacked and killed children in the fields and vineyards, devouring their raw flesh. He was sometimes seen in human shape, sometimes as a "loup-garou." During the sixteenth century in France lycanthropy was very prevalent, and cannibalism was rife in many county districts.

Montague Summers: Note to the fifteenth century *Malleus Maleficarum* which became the Bible of witchfinders across Europe

According to Job Fincel (sixteenth century author of several Books of Marvels) there was a famous case of lycanthropy involving a peasant living near Pavia in Italy in 1541 who was convinced not only that he became a wolf when the madness took him, but that he appeared as such to others, which seems not to have been the case according to several witnesses of his rages. When he was finally caught after savagely attacking many people in the fields, he firmly maintained that he was a true wolf except that his fur grew inwards. His interrogators investigated by cutting deeply into in his body in several places and proved him wrong, but the madman died of his injuries a few days later.

The so-called Werewolf of Chalons, also known as the Demon Tailor,s was convicted for murder in Paris on 14 December 1598. His crimes were so appalling that the court ordered all records destroyed, but surviving rumours said that he used to lure children into his shop and after sexually abusing them would cut their throats and then chop them up like a butcher into joints of meat. Barrels of bleached human bones were found in his cellar. He was also (and perhaps more fancifully) said to prowl the woods at dusk in the form of a wolf and tear out the throats of passing travellers. He was burned to death, unrepentant and blaspheming to the end.

Also in 1598 two countrymen came upon two wolves feeding on the corpse of a teenage boy in a wood near Caude, in the region of Angers, France. To their horror, one of them recognised the boy as his own son. They chased the wolves and lost them, but found instead a wild looking man, half naked with long matted hair and beard, and fingernails like claws that were stained with fresh blood and clogged with flesh.

This man turned out to be a well-known beggar called Jaques Roulet. He spontaneously confessed to having killed the boy with the intention of eating him but had run off when the men arrived. The two wolves he claimed to have been his brother Jean and cousin Julien who, like him, were able to take wolf shape by means of a salve their parents had given them.

On investigation Roulet's parents turned out to be perfectly respectable non-sorcerers and able to prove that Jean and Julien had been elsewhere on the day of the murder. The court sentenced Jaques Roulet to death but on appeal the Paris Parliament commuted this to two years in a madhouse where he was to be 'reaffirmed in his Christian faith', which was believed enough to cure him.

The renowned sixteenth century Dutch physician Petrus Forestus examined a peasant at Alcmaar who was seized by a kind of madness every spring, running round the church and cemetery. He carried a staff to fend off the dogs that always attacked him, but was covered with scars nevertheless. His face was pale and his eyes hollow. Forestus diagnosed him as a lycanthropist, though there was no suggestion that his shape changed during his fits.

Among the ancient Romans 'versipellis', meaning 'reversed skin' was a common form of abuse implying lycanthropy.

The historian Fincelius recorded that in 1542 Constantinople was besieged by werewolves and that the Emperor and his guard killed a hundred and fifty of them.

By the village of Dodow near Wittenburg in Germany is a rise called Fox Hill in memory of the strange fate of a local schoolmaster long ago. One day in class they were discussing magic and one of the pupils said that her grandmother had a magic belt that changed her into a fox whenever she chose. As a result they were never short of geese, chickens and other fresh meat.

The teacher was naturally curious and asked the child to bring the fox strap in to show him – which she did the next day. Unfortunately, while examining the belt, the teacher accidentally put it on and, right in front of his class, turned into a fox. In the following uproar, the fox panicked and jumped clear through the window in a wild leap. That was the last that was seen of the teacher till a great foxhunt a while later. When one fox was shot, it transformed under the startled hunters' eyes back into the missing teacher, so the hill where he had lived as a fox was named in his honour.

In a meadow overlooking Seehausen near the village of Eggensted in the Magdeberg region of Germany is a rocky cliff called Wolf Rock, or sometimes Werewolf Rock and it got its name this way, as told to the Brothers Grimm around 1817:

Long ago a stranger made his home in the Brandsleber Forest near Eggensted. He was called simply 'The Old Man' because no-one knew his true name. He made his living by touring the villages and working as a labourer, most commonly as a shepherd. One day he was hired to shear the flock of a shepherd called Melle from Neindorf. At the end of the day Melle found everything in order except that there was no sign of either The Old Man or a particularly pretty spotted lamb.

For a long time after that there was no sign of The

Old Man till one day as Melle was watching his flock, he reappeared and said sarcastically: "Hello, Melle, your spotted lamb sends its greetings!"

Furious, the farmer attacked The Old Man but suddenly he changed into a wolf and attacked the farmer instead. Luckily his sheepdogs came to the rescue and the werewolf ran off. They chased it through the woods till finally, cornered, the werewolf changed back into human form and begged for mercy – but Melle was having none of it and drove him off the edge of the cliff that bears the wolf's name to this day.

ANOTHER OF THE MOST FAMOUS and best documented werewolf trials was that of thirteen-year-old Jean Grenier in 1603. Grenier was a ragamuffin and scavenger living in the south of France on the Atlantic coast. He was the son of a poor labourer in the village of S. Antoine de Pizon and had taken to wandering the countryside begging and doing odd jobs here and there, often tending sheep. He was in the habit of doing this with young Marguerite Poirier. She was afraid of him but her parents just thought she was being silly. Then one day when she was alone she was attacked by a strange wolf-like creature. It had torn her dress and drawn blood, but she had fought it off with her crook and then run home, abandoning her sheep.

She told her parents that Jean Grenier had often said he could change into a wolf and was especially fond of the flesh of young girls. Enquiries were made and it was found that Grenier had been scaring other girls with the same tale. He was brought in for questioning by the Parliament of Bordeaux.

King James 1 of England shared the view (as declared in his book *Daemonologie* 1597) of lycanthropy being a delusion caused by 'superabundance of melancholic'; though he was fully convinced of the reality of shape-shifting witches turning into cats, foxes and hares.

> *"Lycanthropia, which Avicenna calls Cucubuth, others Lupinam Insaniam or Wolf-Madness, when men run howling about graves and fields in the night, and will not be persuaded but that they are*

Grenier immediately and freely confessed to being a werewolf, saying he had been inducted two or three years before by a satanic being he called the Lord of the Forest, who had given him an ointment and a wolf-skin that let him change into a wolf whenever he chose. He also confessed to several specific instances in which he had attacked and often murdered and eaten children, which was supported by evidence on the ground. He said he would have eaten Marguerite Poirier if she had not defended herself so vigorously.

She was the only one of the surviving witnesses who described him as actually looking much like a wolf, however, and in a landmark decision the court decided that lycanthropy was a delusion of madness and so the boy would only be tried for the murders themselves, not for being a werewolf. He was sentenced to permanent imprisonment in a monastery in Bordeaux where he pined like a wild animal and died by the age of twenty.

THE MOST FAMOUS TRIAL and execution of a werewolf was in Bedburg, near Cologne (Köln) in Germany in 1589, thanks to a famous chapbook or pamphlet of the day that spread the tale across Europe.

This tells how the region suffered for years from what seemed a peculiarly savage wolf that attacked both humans and livestock, dismembering them and scattering their parts around the countryside. People hardly dare travel alone, even by day and if anyone went missing it was assumed the wolf had taken them.

Finally however some villagers managed to corner the beast with dogs whereupon (according to the legend), before their very eyes it transformed into a middle-aged man they recognized as a long-time neighbour, Stubbe Peeter (or Peter Stump,

Stumpf, Stube and a variety of other spellings). First they dragged him to his house to make sure he was not some kind of uncanny double, and then before the local magistrate for questioning.

Threatened with the rack, Peeter quickly confessed to a string of atrocities over 25 years, telling how as a youth he had turned to sorcery and made a pact with the devil, who had given him an enchanted belt by means of which he could change into a wolf to carry out his crimes. A search was made for this belt at the place where he had been caught but there was no trace left of it . . .

Stubbe Peeter confessed to at least sixteen murders, including two pregnant women, whose unborn babies' hearts he considered a special delicacy. Worst of all perhaps, he confessed to the murder of his own beloved son in a fit of bloodlust, enticing him into the countryside and eating his brains.

He was condemned to an agonizing death on 28 October 1589, being tortured and broken on a wheel before finally being beheaded and burned. His daughter and a mistress who were deemed accomplices in some of the murders were burned with him and a monument was raised to the event. The torture wheel was raised on a pole with the likeness of a wolf on it, plus Stubbe Peeter's own head. Sixteen strips of wood were hung from the wheel to commemorate his known victims.

wolves or some such beasts. Aetius and Paulus call it a kind of melancholy; but I should rather refer to it as madness, as most do. This malady is nowadays frequent in Bohemia and Hungary. Schernitzius will have it common in Livonia. They lie hid most part all day, and go abroad in the night, barking, howling, at graves and deserts; they have usually hollow eyes, scabbed legs and thighs, unquenchable thirst and are very dry and pale."

Robert Burton *Anatomy of Melancholy* 1621

In 1685 the Bavarian town of Ansbach, Germany, was terrorized by a wolf said to have killed a large number of women, children, and domestic animals. The rumour spread that it was a werewolf, a revenant of the town's hated Burgomeister who had recently died. Finally some hunters cornered the beast they thought responsible and chased it into a well where it drowned. Hauling out the carcass, the townsfolk dressed the wolf up as the Burgomeister with mask and beard and hung it from a gibbet where it remained for a while before being put on display in the town museum as proof of the reality of werewolves. There's no mention of whether they thought to check his grave at any point to see if he had risen from it.

In 1995 the Ansbach 'werewolf' appeared in an exhibition of curiosities organized by the *Fortean Times* at the Clocktower Museum in Croydon, England.

THE BENANDANTI WOLVES

Werewolves have not always been hostile to humans, according to a curious train of events leading up to startling claims by a self-confessed werewolf in Livonia on the Baltic Sea.

It began over a hundred years earlier with the Inquisition trial in 1575 of a group of peasants near Venice in Italy who entered folklore as the *benandanti*, which means something like 'those who do good'. These peasants, male and female, had all been born with a caul (amniotic sac) over their heads, widely considered a warning of those who will later become werewolves, vampires or sorcerers. This gave them supernatural powers which they claimed to use four times a year at the turn of the seasons to do battle with witches for the success of the year's crops.

Prosecutions continued for the next 70 years but they were very mild by the standards of the Inquisition elsewhere, possibly because of hostility towards the Inquisition from the Venetian authorities. As long as the peasants accepted the error of their ways (trying to use magic instead of prayer) and agreed to change them, they were dismissed and there is no record of any executions.

The legend of the *benandanti* seems to have inspired remarkable testimony given at a trial in Jurgenburg, Livonia, in 1692. The defendant, an 80-year-old-man named Theiss, freely admitted to being a werewolf but claimed that he and many other werewolves actually helped farmers by battling with witches and warlocks who would otherwise cause the crops to fail.

Three nights a year he said, on the feasts of St Lucia, Pentecost and St John, the turning points of the seasons, the werewolves descended to hell to battle the witches, wielding iron bars against their broomsticks. Theiss claimed that his own broken nose had come from a dead warlock called Skeistan, whose broom handle had been wrapped in a horse's tail.

Theiss insisted that he and his kind were the "Hounds of God" and that they would go to heaven after death. He also claimed there were many other bands of witch-fighting werewolves in Germany and Russia who likewise went down to hell to defend the crops. Theiss denied ever having dealt with the devil and refused to see a parish priest sent to correct his theology, saying he was a better man than any priest.

The court was baffled to know what to make of this confession and finally sentenced Theiss to ten lashes for blasphemy and superstition.

THE BEAST OF GAVAUDIN

In the summer of 1764 a strange monster was seen in a mountainous part of the Gavaudin province in southern central France (now part of the Auvergne region). Then a girl was killed and the heart ripped from her body. Other sightings and savage killings followed, usually involving the head being crushed.

One witness, a girl who survived an early attack by the beast in the Merçoire forest near Langogne, described it as the size of a donkey and wolf-like, though enormous. She further said it had ears that looked like pointed horns, long fangs and a black stripe running from its head

THE TOWN OF Wittlich (now Bernkastel-Wittlich) is reputed to be the last place in Germany where a werewolf was killed. The story goes that after Napoleon's disastrous defeat at Moscow in 1812 there was mass desertion from his army. One such deserter was Thomas Johannes Baptist Schwytzer who happened to pass Wittlich on his way home to Alsace. With him were a number of Russian deserters he had befriended. Being hungry, they decided to raid a farm and, when caught by the farmer and his sons, murdered the lot.

Witnessing this, the distraught farmer's wife screeched a curse at Schwytzer just before he crushed her skull: "From this day forth with each full moon you will change into a rabid wolf!"

The curse seemed to work because from that time Schwytzer grew steadily more savage, especially at times of the full moon. His robberies, rapes and murders grew so indiscriminate that his friends abandoned him. He took up with bandits and highwaymen but even they could not stomach his

excesses so finally he roamed the wild forests alone. Rumours began to spread of a werewolf on the prowl as humans and cattle were savaged.

One night Schwytzer cornered and raped Elizabeth Beierle, a beautiful farmer's daughter. Suspicion fell on him as the werewolf and when some villagers caught him by a campfire soon afterwards, they chased and cornered him near the village of Morbach. They killed and buried him at a crossing where a shrine was built, with a candle that was never allowed to go out. Local legend held that if it did, the werewolf would return.

Elizabeth Beierle gave birth later to a child she named Martin, and their descendants have thrived as respectable citizens ever since, with no sign of being tainted by Thomas Johannes Baptist Schwytzer's savagery. The legend and the shrine have also persisted, with a curious modern twist.

On a night in 1988 a group of American servicemen passed it on their way to the Morbach munitions base nearby. They noticed that the candle was out and joked about the danger of werewolves. Later that same night though, the perimeter alarms at the Morbach base were triggered and one of the investigating guards claimed to see a huge 'dog-like' creature which stood up on its hind legs and looked at him before leaping easily over the two or three metre chain-link fence. A guard dog brought to the spot seemed overcome with terror . . .

to the tip of its tail. Its clawed paws were larger than a man's hands and its eyes bright red. It ran very fast but in leaps and bounds. It tried twice to attack her as she was tending cattle but the bulls in her herd drove it off, leaving her no more than scratched and shaken.

Hunters went into action and in October two of them shot it from a distance of only thirty feet but the wounded creature escaped them and within a few days was killing again. This apparently supernatural escape convinced people it was no ordinary wolf but a *loup garou.*

After more children were horribly killed the matter came to the attention of King Louis XV who sent a troop of cavalry to hunt the monster down. They spotted it many times and possibly shot it, though no body was found. The beast did disappear for a while though and, assuming it had died somewhere in a hole, the cavalry withdrew. Soon afterwards the killings began again.

A large bounty was posted, attracting hundreds of professional hunters. They killed over a hundred common wolves but none was the Beast, which continued to roam and kill as it pleased for the next two years despite being occasionally injured.

Finally in June 1767 the Marquis d'Apcher organised over 300 hunters and beaters into disciplined groups to comb the countryside. One party cornered the Beast and the hero of the day was one Jean Chastel who fired two rifle shots and his second silver bullet pierced the beast's heart and killed it.

In the beast's stomach was found a young girl's collar bone and it was credited with up to a hundred deaths and thirty maimings. The survivors were said to have mostly gone mad after their ordeal. The beast's body was put on public display and even taken to Versailles before eventually being buried and lost to modern investigation.

Despite being so publicly laid to rest, the legend of the Beast of Gavaudin has been kept fresh by later sightings of a similar creature in the same area even down to the present day. In 2001 the film *Brotherhood of the Wolf* helped revive interest in the beast while taking many liberties with known facts.

CANNIBALISM

Cannibalism is an intrinsic element of lycanthropy. The motive of the attacks is very rarely gain, revenge or any of the other usual reasons for murder. The chief aim is to eat raw and preferably human flesh.

Although cannibalism is usually associated with horror, it is not always predatory. It used to be the custom with the Biblinga tribe in Australia (among many others around the world) to eat their own dead to ensure their reincarnation within the tribe.

One of the most famous cannibals in British history was Sawney Beane (see box) whose notorious clan terrified the Galloway coast in Scotland during the reign James VI (James I of England) 1566 - 1625. He and his brood combined a taste for human flesh with self interest by robbing and eating passers-by.

On a smaller scale than Sawney Beane but no less horrific in its own way was the cannibal family found in 1849 in Galicia, in what is now southern Poland. In the area of Polomyja, one of many tiny villages scattered through the vast pine forests, children began to go missing.

In the bitter winter of that year wolves also became a menace to livestock and the two were connected – people assumed the wolves were taking the children and began killing any they could find. Then in May of that year the innkeeper of Polomyja found a couple of his ducks missing. Suspecting a beggar named Swiatek who lived with his family nearby, the innkeeper decided to investigate.

Approaching the beggar's cottage, he smelt succulent roasting meat. Convinced now of his suspicions, the innkeeper burst in. As the door flew open, he saw Swiatek kick something on the floor out of sight beneath his robe. Hauling the man aside, the innkeeper was then horrified by a girl's head that rolled into view, fourteen or fifteen years old.

Swiatek and his wife, sixteen-year-old daughter and five-year-old-son were locked up and the cottage searched. The remains of several more children were found, neatly prepared and stored ready for eating.

At his trial Swiatek claimed his taste for human flesh was first excited three years before by the discovery of a burned corpse. It belonged to a Jewish innkeeper whose premises had been set on fire. As he was starving at the time, Swiatek was tempted to try the flesh and enjoyed it so much it started him on his new career – luring away children and killing them for meat. He confessed to six murders but his children said there had been many more and there was evidence of up to fourteen victims at the cottage.

The authorities feared a lynching when the news got out but Swiatek saved everyone the trouble by hanging himself from the bars of his cell.

TRAVELLERS' TALES

The French author George Sand wrote in 1858 that she knew: "several persons who at the first faint rising of the new moon have met near the carfax of the Croix-Blanche old Soupison, nicknamed *Demmonet*, walking swiftly along with great giant strides followed in silence by more than thirty wolves".

SAWNEY BEANE grew up as the child of peasants in a village a few miles east of Edinburgh. His father was a hedger and ditcher and for a while Sawney also followed this trade, though not very successfully. Then he ran off with his woman to a deserted part of the Galloway coast where they made their home in a cave that was supposed to run about a mile under the ground and whose entrance was submerged at high tide. Here they stayed for the next quarter century without visiting any town or city.

In the cave they bred children and (incestuously) grandchildren that they trained in their trade, which was to murder passing travellers – man, woman or child – that they robbed and then butchered, human flesh being their main source of food. Other than this they had no contact with outsiders and left no survivors so that the very existence of the unholy tribe long remained unknown, even though the disappearance of travellers was noticed and body parts washed up along the coast.

Fewer and fewer people dared travel the roads except in large groups and several innkeepers were

executed on suspicion of murdering their guests. But still the killings continued until finally the Beanes' luck ran out.

A man was riding home one evening from a fair with his wife mounted behind him when they fell into an ambush by the Beane clan. The man was armed with sword and pistol and put up a stiff fight. But his wife fell off the horse and was murdered under his eyes, having her throat bitten and her intestines pulled out. Just then some two dozen other fairgoers came along and rescued him, putting the attackers to flight. That lucky man was the first known victim to survive.

A few days later the King himself arrived at the scene with 300 men and the whole countryside was searched. Luckily the tide was out when the King's party passed the cave mouth on the shore. But even then the searchers might have passed it by had not some bloodhounds investigated and set up a howl of alarm. Torches were found and the caves searched until finally the cannibals' nest was found. Human limbs lined the walls like hams or had been pickled. Piles of gold silver, jewellery, weapons and other pickings from the victims were found.

At the time of capture, Sawney Beane's family consisted of his wife, eight sons, six daughters, eighteen grandsons, and fourteen granddaughters, who were 'all begotten in incest', as one broadsheet put it. It was estimated that they may have claimed up to a thousand travellers in their 25 year reign. There was no formal trial. The Beanes were marched to Leith where the males had their arms and legs cut off under the eyes of their women and left to die. The women were then burned alive in three fires and were said to have died spitting and cursing to the end.

George Sand's artist son Maurice painted and drew many werewolves including the lupins or lubins below. In Normandy these were said to stand by the walls of rural cemeteries chatting in a strange tongue and occasionally howling at the moon. They are harmless and will scatter at the approach of humans.

Montague Summers in *The Werewolf* 1933 tells the story of a phantom werewolf haunting in Scotland in the 1880s. An Oxford professor and his wife had taken a holiday cottage by one of the remoter lakes of Merionethshire. One day while wading out into the waters to fish, the professor stumbled on a skull which he took to belong to a very large dog. He set it on the kitchen shelf that night for later examination before going out with a friend, leaving his wife alone in the cottage.

After dark she heard animal noises by the kitchen door, like those of a large dog. She went to check the door was bolted and was met with a large half-human, half-beast glaring in at her through the window. Panic followed as she flew to lock the back door and then the front and then cowered in terror while the beast prowled round the cottage trying ways to get in.

In *Travels in Portugal* 1875 author John Latouche (a pen name) told the tale of a recent werewolf, which he heard from an old man who claimed to have been closely involved with the incident in his youth. In fact he (the old man) had been responsible for introducing the werewolf into the household where he was working as a wealthy farmer's servant. The mistress of the house being about to give birth, he had been sent to Ponte de Lima, the nearest town to recruit a housekeeper.

By chance he met a young woman called Joana on the way who seemed to fit the requirements perfectly. So he brought her home and she appeared to settle in happily, apart maybe from occasionally showing a fierce temper to fellow servants.

All went well; the baby was born a fine healthy boy who seemed perfect in every way. But when they showed him to a local wise-woman she told them that the child was under a curse and even found a birthmark shaped like a crescent moon between its shoulders. However, she reassured them that all they needed do to protect the baby was guard its cradle closely at each new moon when it was most vulnerable. This was done and the next few months passed without incident.

Then Joana informed her mistress that there was a better way to lift the curse, and it was also the only way to prevent the child becoming a werewolf at sixteen. The birthmark was to be anointed with the blood of a white pigeon and the babe then laid naked on a hillside on the first night that a new moon rose after midnight.

After much debate within the family it was decided to follow this advice and the next time the moon reached the right phase all was done as Joana suggested. Everyone retired home, leaving the child alone on the hillside under the crescent moon, which was needed for the charm to work. Shortly however they heard screaming and rushed out into the night again, the father armed with a big blunderbuss. They ran to the spot and to their horror found an enormous wolf standing over the child with blood dripping from its jaws.

The farmer fired his gun and a servant attacked it with a club, almost breaking its foreleg before it escaped wounded into the shadows. The baby had had its life ripped out of it.

The next day when they searched the area they found the housekeeper Joana lying in bushes not far from the scene dying from a gunshot wound and a badly mangled arm. She tried to claim these wounds came from trying to defend the child against the beast and in charity they sent for the priest to give her the last rites, but she died before he arrived.

Finally her husband and his friend returned and the noise of their arrival drove the spectre away. After hearing the wife's tale the two men decided to sit up in wait, armed with a gun and stout cudgels. Finally they were rewarded by a faint noise outside and then scratching at the kitchen window. Framed in the window was the glaring head of a wolf. Before they could shoot, it spotted them and ran. They raced out into the night after it and saw a huge animal disappearing into the lake without a ripple. The next day they rowed out into the lake and threw the skull into its deepest part. And their nights were not troubled again.

REAL WOLF PEOPLE

Throughout history there have been accounts of people such as the Babylonian King Nebuchadnezzar who when living wild have begun to resemble wild animals with hair growing all over their bodies. This also happens with some feral children and is a known side-effect of certain kinds of malnutrition, such as eating only raw meat, which would follow from living with wolves.

There are also people born that way with a condition known as hypertrichosis (literally – extreme hairiness) in which hair grows all over the body and especially the face, giving sufferers the look of the classic movie werewolf. The chances of this happening are estimated at about one in ten billion, but the condition is often then passed from parents to children.

One of the most famous wolf men in history thanks to some fine paintings in the Ambras Art Collection in Vienna, is Petrus Gonsalvus, known as the Wolf Man of the Canary Islands. Born in 1556 in Tenerife, he was brought as a child to the French court of Henry II who personally supervised his education as a man of culture. Later he moved to Flanders under the patronage of Margaret of Parma, regent of the Netherlands. There he married and two of his children, a boy and girl, shared his condition. This made them popular subjects for medical research, being examined by, among others, Felix Plater of Basel and Ulysses Aldrovandi of Bologna who have left detailed records. Portraits and descriptions of their lives are also to be found in the 1582 sketchbook of Georg Hoefnagel in the Austrian National Library, Vienna.

The nineteenth century wolf man Adrian Jeftichew came from the Caucasus Mountains in Russia. He toured Europe and grew quite rich on the proceeds but believed that his condition had doomed him to damnation. His son Fedor was born in 1868 in St Petersburg with the same condition and toured with

his father as Jo-jo the Wolf Boy. When his father died he signed with P.T. Barnum who took him to the US at the age of 16 where he was an enormous success, becoming probably the most famous Wolf Man in carnival history and helping to inspire the look of wolf men a while later in Hollywood.

In keeping with his circus persona's myth of having grown up wild in the Russian forests before being caught by a hunter in Kostromo, Jo-jo only growled and barked on stage but in private he spoke three or four languages fluently and was highly intelligent. He died from pneumonia in Turkey in 1904.

In the early 2000s two acrobats became famous in the Mexican National Circus as the Wolf Boys. Larry and

Danny Ramos Gomez come from the Aceves family from the remote mountain town of Zacatecas that carries a strain of hypertrichosis. In their cases and that of at least one cousin their faces and bodies are as hairy as Jo-jo's, while in others it is much less pronounced or even absent altogether. Some relations shave and pass unnoticed in crowds while others, like the Boys, are defiantly proud of their condition despite the superstitious hostility or revulsion it often prompts (it's not unusual for people to cross themselves or the road and make other warding gestures against bad luck when meeting them on the street).

When diva actress and world beauty Elizabeth Taylor was born she suffered from residual hypertrichosis, having a soft mat of dark hair all over her body and "her ears were covered with thick, black fuzz and inlaid into the sides of her head," her mother once admitted. Luckily for her future career this condition soon passed naturally.

FERAL CHILDREN

Ever since Romulus and Remus there have been tales of lost children being brought up by wild animals, most commonly wolves, which suggests a natural affinity, even if the relationship did become poisoned at some time, most probably when humans settled down to farming. At which point the wolf came to be seen as an enemy instead of just an admirable rival in the hunt, which appears to have been the early hunter-gatherers' attitude towards it.

Here are just a few typical examples of wolf-reared children from the scores on record:

In the *Arcana Microcosmi* by Alexander Ross (1652, bk2 ch4) is a brief, second-hand account of a French wolf boy, "*a childe that was carried away in the Forest of Ardenne by Wolves, and nourished by them. This child having conversed with them divers years, was at last apprehended, but could neither speak nor walk upright, nor eat any thing except raw flesh, till by a new education among other children, his bestial nature was quite abolished*".

Lippincott's Magazine (1898, vol LXI; p121) carried this story: "*Also Mr. Greig, late of the 93 rd (Sutherland) Highlanders declares that when his regiment was marching toward Bareilly in 1858, after the taking of Lucknow, he saw at Shahjehenpur an individual said to have been, as a child, taken away from his village by wolves, brought up by them, and to have lived with them for several years. He appeared to be about twenty years of age; his body was covered with short brown hair; his powers of speech extended to nothing beyond low grunts, and he could not be induced to wear any kind of clothing. Whenever he saw raw meat he rushed for it and devoured it greedily. The story was that he had been ridden down and caught by a native after a long chase, and that he did not run on his feet like a human being, but on all fours like an animal.*"

IN 1920 Rev Joseph Singh, a missionary who ran an orphanage in northern India, heard rumours of two 'ghosts' while touring his district in the area of Midnapore in the Bengal jungle. They were said to accompany a band of wolves and had all the locals terrified. Singh had a hide built in a tree overlooking a place they were commonly seen – a tall white-ant hill with several large entrances.

At dusk suddenly a wolf emerged from the hill, followed by two others and then two wolf cubs. Then came the 'ghosts', two strange looking creatures that were vaguely human-seeming but which ran on all fours, had large balls of fur over their heads and shoulders and very bright eyes.

A few days later the missionary returned with a team of diggers. At the first few shovel blows two large wolves burst from the mound and fled into the jungle. Then came a third, the mother wolf, which attacked the diggers furiously and could not be driven away. So they killed it with arrows. Within the hollowed out ant hill they found two wolf cubs, which the diggers sold at market, and two human girls that the Reverend Singh took back to his orphanage.

The girl's ages were guessed about eight and one and a half and they were named Kamala and Amala. As nearly as possible they behaved just like wolves. They hated clothes and by choice would eat only raw meat and milk. They were also unable to stand upright and unable to interact with the other children at the orphanage. Amala, the younger one, died about a year after her capture. Kamala lived much longer and gradually acquired some normal human characteristics, learned to walk upright and formed an affectionate bond with Mrs Singh, but after several years still only had a vocabulary of about forty words. Whether she could ever totally adapt to being human was never tested because nine years after her capture she caught typhoid and died.

In May 1972 Narsing Bahadur Singh, headman of the village of Narangpur twenty miles or so from Sultanpur in Uttar Pradesh, India, came upon a wild boy playing with four or five wolf cubs. Although he ran quickly on all fours, Singh captured him easily enough and took him home, naming him Shamdeo.

On capture, Shamdeo had very dark skin, matted hair, finger- and toenails resembling claws and thick calluses on his hands, elbows and knees. He hid from sunlight and became restless at night. He also became excited by the smell of blood and caught chickens which he ate raw, including the entrails. In short he behaved just like a wolf and was unable to talk.

The village headman held onto Shamdeo for about five months till he escaped and lived by scavenging around the village till he was taken into an orphanage run by Mother Teresa's Mission of Charity. At first he would rip off his clothes and throw away cooked food, but gradually he is said to have settled in to orphanage life. Author Bruce Chatwin visited him there to check out the story, and by this time the boy was using rudimentary sign language and the calluses had gone from his knees and elbows.

CHAPTER III

Shadows in the Night: Werewolves in Fiction

Many werewolf stories have been written over the centuries, shaping the popular view of these monsters, but they have not yet crystallised into any monumental classic equivalent to, say, *Dracula* in relation to vampires or Mary Shelley's *Frankenstein* in relation to, well, Frankenstein monsters.

A very popular early rhymed romance was *Bisclavret* by Marie de France, a twelfth century poet in England who was possibly a half sister to King Henry II. *Bisclavret* is the Breton word for werewolf and the story tells of a great lord in Brittany who troubles his loving wife by his habit of disappearing for three whole days each week without explanation.

Finally she teases the truth out of him and he confesses that for those three days he wanders in the depths of the forest as a werewolf, living by violence and blood. He has to be naked for this and eventually she coaxes from him the secret of where he hides his clothes, without which he is unable to change back into a man.

A while later the wife falls in love with someone else and persuades her lover to steal her lord's clothes while he is away so he is doomed to remain a wolf. In due course he is declared dead and his wife marries her lover but, this being a fairytale, they do not live happily ever after. After many adventures the werewolf finally succeeds in making the truth known and, his clothes having luckily not been destroyed, is able to resume human form and exact vengeance.

An interesting point about *Bisclavret* is that there is no censure of the lord for being a werewolf, presumably because he only attacked animals. He is the righteous party in the fable.

Another case of a noble werewolf in twelfth century romantic poetry is *The Romance of William of Palermo* or *William and the Werewolf* whose popularity was continued as a prose version in the sixteenth century.

The tale is rather long and complicated but at the heart of it is that young William, Prince of Apulia, is snatched away as a child by a seemingly ravening wolf. It swims with him in its jaws from Sicily to Italy and then to a forest near Rome where, far from making a meal of him, the wolf nurtures William tenderly and raises him to a young man, later helping in the adventures that lead to him becoming Emperor of Rome. It turns out that the wolf is a prince under enchantment who had saved William from a plot to kill him. This Prince Alphonsus finally recovers human form to become King of Spain.

John Webster's Jacobean play *The Duchess of Malfi* has a werewolf in the form of the heroine's tormented twin brother, whose lycanthropy is suggested to have been brought on by melancholy; but this is not central to the story.

Other novels and plays also introduced lycanthropy as spice to their plot. In the nineteenth century tales like *Hugues, the Wer-Wolf* by Sutherland Menzies (1838), *Wagner the Wehr-Wolf* (1846) by George W. M. Reynolds, *The Wehr-Wolf of Wilton Crescent* 1855 by Dudley Costello and *The Wolf-Leader* (1857) by Alexander Dumas familiarised readers with the concept; but none took the world by storm or are commonly read today.

One of the most influential novels in fact was not a werewolf story at all. *The Strange Case of Dr Jekyll and Mr Hyde* (1886) by Robert Louis Stevenson perfectly captures the predicament of the 'involuntary werewolf' whose savage fits are beyond conscious control. This book probably did more than any other to pave the way for the werewolf's popularity in the cinema.

LITTLE RED RIDING HOOD

The most famous werewolf story of all is the children's fable of Little Red Riding Hood. Usually the beast is described simply as a wolf but consciously or unconsciously this has long been read as 'werewolf'.

This is explicit in the French folk tale *The Story of a Grandmother collected* by Achille Millien in the Nivernais region of the Loire valley in 1870, but almost certainly much older. Here the villain is actually called a *bzou* – a kind of werewolf. In this version when the little girl finds herself in bed with the wolf, she claims the sudden need to relieve herself. The *bzou* tells her to do it in the bed but she says: "Oh no, because that would smell bad!" so the lazy wolf ties her ankle to a leash and lets her out of the cottage. Once outside, she ties it to a tree and makes her escape.

The story of Little Red Riding Hood was first published by Charles Perrault in Paris in 1697 accompanied by an engraving showing the wolf climbing into bed on top of the girl. In the French slang of the day, when a girl lost her virginity she was said to have 'seen the wolf'.

In Perrault's tale the girl is eaten by the wolf and it ends with the warning that: "Children, especially attractive, well bred young ladies, should never talk to strangers, for if they should do so, they may well provide dinner for a wolf."

Her and her grandmother's rescue from the wolf by a passing woodcutter was introduced into the Brothers Grimm version of 1812.

The French for hood is 'chaperon' which also means, as it came to mean in English, a guardian of virtue.

From being an emblem of helpless and endangered female innocence, Little Red riding Hood has evolved into a proactive symbol of feminine assertion. In 1953 Max Factor cosmetics launched 'Red Riding Hood' lipstick with the promise that it would 'bring out the wolves'. Other cosmetics firms have periodically repeated this promise ever since, including Chanel in 1999 whose glossy Red Riding Hood video commercial was scored by Danny Elfman who has orchestrated many fantasy blockbusters including Harry Potter and Spiderman.

Angela Carter co-scripted the 1984 movie *The Company of Wolves* based on her short story in *Bloody Chamber* 1979, a feminist retelling of Perrault's fairytales. In the movie the girl becomes a wolf herself and takes bloody revenge on her would-be stalker.

In the 1996 movie *Freeway* Reese Witherspoon plays a tough runaway girl in a red leather jacket who runs into a serial killer while hitching her way to her granny's trailer park. In the modern tradition she proves more than a match for him.

LANDMARK WEREWOLF MOVIES

As with *Dracula* the cinema is mainly responsible for the werewolf's popular image. The closest there is to a classic werewolf novel is Guy Endore's *Werewolf of Paris* 1933 which has directly inspired many films including *The Werewolf of London* (Universal Studios,1935) *The Curse of the Werewolf* (Hammer Films, 1961) and *The Legend of the Werewolf* (Tyburn Films, 1974).

There have been far too many werewolf movies for more than a brief subjective listing here, but these are just a few that are outstanding for one reason or another:

◆ 1913 *The Werewolf*
Generally recognized as the first werewolf movie to make an impact, this silent classic used a real wolf in the transformation scene.

◆ 1932 *Le Loup Garou*
German film, first werewolf movie with sound.

◆ 1931 *Dr Jekyll & Mr Hyde*
Starring Frederic March, Miriam Hopkins and Rose Hobart, this was the classic pre-war adaptation of Stevenson's tale produced in a vintage year that also saw classic versions of *Dracula* and *Frankenstein.*

◆ 1935 *The Werewolf of London*
First werewolf film by Universal Studios. Notable for being the first werewolf movie in which the character does not simply change into a wolf but a man-wolf hybrid, heavily influenced by Jekyll and Hyde but with an interesting twist of the story beginning in Tibet.

◆ 1941 *The Wolf Man*
Directed by George Waggoner and starring Lon Chaney Jr, this Universal film clearly established the guidelines for fictional werewolves, encapsulated in this now famous rhyme:

Even a man who is pure in heart
And says his prayers at night
May become a wolf when the wolf-bane blooms
And the autumn moon is bright.

This film also popularised the notion that the werewolf is only vulnerable to silver weapons or bullets.

◆ 1941 *Dr Jekyll & Mr Hyde*
Directed by Victor Fleming, this film finally dislodged the 1931 classic with an all star cast headed by Spencer Tracy, Ingrid Bergman and Lana Turner.

◆ 1957 *I Was a Teenage Werewolf*
Stars Michael Landon in the title role as a kid with a temper problem who seeks help from a doctor who is more interested in experimenting than curing him. Directed by Gene Fowler Jr.

◆ 1961 *Curse of the Werewolf*
This Hammer Films classic launched the career of Oliver Reed and also starred Warren Mitchell, Clifford Evans, Yvonne Romain and Catherine Feller.
An adaption of Guy Endore's 1933 novel *Werewolf of Paris*.

◆ 1974 *Legend of the Werewolf*
Directed by Freddie Francis and one of three Tyburn

Films productions that aimed to steal some of Hammer's limelight just when Hammer's period of glory was passing. Closely based on and with the same scriptwriter as Hammer's *Curse of the Werewolf* (see above).

◆ 1975 *Ilsa: She Wolf of the SS*
Classic sexploitation movie of the '70s in astonishingly bad taste, starring Dianne Thorne and directed by Don Edmonds. The producer David Friedman was apparently so shocked by the results that he changed his name in the credits to Herman Traeger. Despite (or perhaps because of) being damnable on almost every front, it continues to enjoy a cult following.

◆ 1981 *An American Werewolf in London*
Directed by John Landis, this film broke several barriers in special effects and includes elements of pathos and dark humour that have won it wide popularity.

◆ 1981 *The Howling*
Directed by Joe Dante, a protégé of Roger Corman and following the same vein of low budget, knowingly humorous wild action, this became an instant cult classic and inspired many imitators. Loosely based on Gary Brandner's novel of the same name.

◆ 1981 *Wolfen*
Based on the 1978 Whitley Streiber novel, this was directed by Michael Wadleigh whose only previous film of note was *Woodstock*, the movie which helped immortalise the event twelve years earlier. This was a mixed success and his last film. Stars Albert Finney and Diane Venora.

◆ 1984 *The Company of Wolves*
Directed by Neil Jordan with a script by Jordan and Angela Carter, this is a retelling of the story of Little Red riding Hood for the modern age.

◆ 1985 *Teen Wolf*
Starring Michael J Fox as a teenager who discovers his family has even more skeletons in the closet than most.

◆ 1994 *Wolf*
Directed by Mike Nichols (*Who's Afraid of Virginia Woolf? The Graduate* and *Catch 22*). Starring Jack Nicholson, Michelle Pfeiffer, James Spader and Christopher Plummer, this is a thoughtful psychological look at lycanthropy with minimal special effects and a mostly restrained performance by Nicholson.

◆ 2004 *Romasanta: The Werewolf Hunt*
Based on true story of Manuel Blanco Romasanta, a travelling salesman who in 1852 confessed to murdering thirteen people and using their fat to make soap. He avoided execution by claiming to be a werewolf in court.

CHAPTER IV

Modern Werewolves

In Argentina and Brazil it is still widely believed that the seventh successive son in a family (without any daughters between) is likely to become a werewolf or *lobison*. In the early twentieth century the idea grew so popular that such boys were abandoned or even killed. So in 1920 the President of Argentina instituted a law whereby he personally became godfather to every seventh son, who also received a gold medal at baptism and a scholarship to the age of 21. The law is still in force today.

In 1920 the fanatical right wing group Operation Werewolf was founded in Germany by Fritz Kappe. In 1923 this group helped create the Nazi party. When Hitler became Chancellor in 1933 one of the titles he gave himself was Father Wolf of the Germanic people. In 1945 when German defeat became inevitable, Goebbels resurrected Operation Werewolf as a terrorist resistance movement. It was also a code name for the final desperate kamikaze raids of the Luftwaffe in 1945. On 7 April, 184

IN THE 1920s rumours of a werewolf began circulating in the German city of Hanover after the discovery of human skulls being washed up from the River Leine. The river was dammed and searched and hundreds more human bones were found, coming from dozens of bodies, all those of young men between the ages of 15 and 20.

Panic gripped the city until finally, more by luck than judgement, suspicion settled on Fritz Haarman, a known black-market trader in meat and clothes who ironically also had a reputation as being a philanthropist towards the penniless young men who drifted into the city in those stricken post-war years.

What Haarman with the aid of his accomplice, young Hans Gras, used to do was befriend homeless young men at the train station and take them home where they would be wined, dined and often bedded. Then Haarman, in his own words, would "throw myself on top of those boys and bite through the Adam's apple, throttling them at the same time".

Afterwards he butchered them, selling their meat and clothes on the street and disposing of their remains in various ways, but most often by simply dumping them in the river. He was convicted of 27 killings though the true number was probably at least twice that. Haarman was beheaded in prison in December 1924 and Gras was also executed.

suicide pilots attacked the American 452nd and 388th Bomber Groups heading for Hanover. 133 planes were lost and only 77 pilots survived. 60 of these died a few days later dive-bombing bridges in the east to slow the Russian advance.

The November 1975 issue of The Canadian Psychiatric Association Journal published several studies of late twentieth century lycanthropy.

One was of a 21-year-old man who was convinced he had become a werewolf. It had begun, he said, while he was serving in the US Army in Germany. One day he had hiked into the forests near his base and taken LSD laced with strychnine, a modern equivalent of the potions mixed by the sorcerers of old. Soon he felt fur growing on his face and claimed to have seen it growing on his hands. Then he felt a compulsion to catch and eat rabbit raw. The fit possessed him for several days before he came to his senses and returned to his post

Medicated with the tranquilizer chlorpromazine, this subject was weaned off other drugs and given therapy for several months, during which time he still complained of being possessed by the devil and having auditory and visual hallucinations. He was diagnosed as suffering from acute schizophrenic or toxic psychosis and was given an antipsychotic drug which seemed to work because he was finally discharged to outpatient treatment. He only attended a couple of times though before disappearing from the record.

Another subject was a 37-year-old vagrant man with wild hair and beard who was admitted to hospital because of disorderly behaviour. This had included howling at the moon, sleeping in cemeteries and lying down in the middle of the road. He had no history of substance abuse and had served in the US Navy where tests had shown him to be of average intelligence. After that he had been a farmer and had seemed quite normal whereas now, besides being psychotic he had the mental age of a child.

A biopsy showed a rare brain disorder known as 'walnut brain' whose cause is unknown but involves physical deterioration of the brain tissue. When given antipsychotic drugs he shed his wild behaviour and became quite docile, though still had only the understanding of a child.

THE BRAY ROAD BEAST

In 1992 the small town of Elkhorn, Wisconsin, became famous for sightings of what became known as the Bray Road Beast. This was a werewolf-like creature seen independently by several witnesses, not just in Bray Road but all over the area. When the story hit the national news others came forward claiming they had not spoken out before for fear of ridicule.

Typical of such eyewitness accounts is this one by Lori Endrizzi of Elkhorn, published in the seminal article by Linda Godfrey (www.cnb-scene.com) in *The Week* Sunday, December 29, 1991:

"Its elbows were up, and its claws were facing out so I knew it had claws. I remember the long claws. And it was eating roadkill or something, and as I drove by and I saw all this, it looked right at me and didn't run. It didn't get spooked, or anything. And it had, like, glowing eyes which probably were a reflection of my headlights. It was right on Bray Road, right before the Bray farm, on the curve. And I saw it. He was brownish-gray... and he had big teeth and fangs. He turned his head to look at me.

"It was about the size of an average man, five-foot-seven maybe, about 150 pounds. It was holding the thing it was eating palms up, with the real long claws and the pointed ears. He had a big long nose and a long chin, like this on this picture [she pointed to a drawing of a 'werewolf' from a library book]. This is exactly what I saw."

The fuss died away, overtaken by other news, but surfaced again in March 1993 in the *Milwaukee Journal* under the headline "Man Found Guilty in Werewolf Trial". The story was about Jose L. Contreras, 45, who was arrested for carrying a handgun and ammunition in public without a license after an Elkhorn resident reported a prowler. Contreras' defence was that he was carrying the gun as protection against the Bray Road Werewolf but (possibly because none of his bullets was silver) this was dismissed.

A full account of the affair can be found at www.weird-wi.com/brayroad

THE OCTOBER 1977 issue of *The American Journal of Psychiatry* tells the tale of a 49-year-old woman whose secret fantasies of wild, bestial behaviour steadily grew during a seemingly normal 20 year marriage till they finally burst into reality in the form of wild behaviour, including stripping naked at a family dinner and making wolf-like sexual advances to her own mother.

The wolf had long been a central figure in her erotic fantasies but now, she said, she began feeling like an animal with claws – felt that she was turning into a wolf. One night after sex with her husband she had a frantic two hour fit of grunting and clawing and chewing things, and said afterwards that the devil had taken over her body.

In hospital she was given medication and therapy but had frequent relapses, especially when the moon was full. In these fits she claimed to see herself as a wolf in the mirror and feel a fierce urge to kill along with intense sexual excitements. Most of the noises she made while possessed were incoherent animal-like grunts and growls, but sometimes she would rave: "I am a wolf of the night. I am wolf woman of the day. I have claws, teeth, fangs, hair and anguish is my prey at night, powerless is my cause. I am what I am and will always roam the earth after death. I will continue to search for perfection and salvation."

After nine weeks of treatment she was released with a program of drugs to control her moods.

In 2004 Germany (and the rest of the world) was stunned by the case of Armin Miewe who was inevitably dubbed the Cannibal of Rotenburg. Miewe was convicted and sentenced to eight years on a charge of manslaughter for the killing and consumption of Bernd Brandes, 43, who had apparently volunteered for the sacrifice. Although not strictly speaking a werewolf since he appears to have acted in complete icy calm, Miewe's cannibalistic urges tie him in to the same stratum of human tendency.

Miewe and Brandes had met on the internet through shared interests in homosexuality, sado-masochism and cannibalism. For Miewe killing and eating another person had been his life's great ambition, but he only considered doing something about it after his domineering mother died in 1999. Then he began converting part of the rambling, 44 roomed, half-timbered and rotting house which he had shared with his mother into the slaughter room of his dreams. Like Norman Bates in *Psycho* he also dressed up in his mother's clothes and kept her room as a shrine, with a dummy head on the pillow.

From around Valentine's Day 2001 Miewes and Brandes conducted a bizarre courtship on the internet which ended with Brandes catching a train to Rotenburg on 9 March. Miewes showed his guest the slaughter room then after having sex they went to the kitchen where, after Brandes had downed a lot of painkillers and alcohol, Miewes chopped off his penis and fried it with garlic for them both to eat. It proved too tough so Brandes was then put in a warm bath to 'bleed out'. Miewe meanwhile read

a Star Trek novel while he waited and after ten hours he dragged his guest to the slaughter room and cut his throat to finish the job. Then he butchered the body and stored the meat in a cellar freezer under boxes of pizza.

The meat lasted Miewe ten months and he was only caught when he began searching the internet for a new volunteer. One correspondent reported him to the police when he realised Miewe was neither joking nor play-acting.

At least three other volunteers visited Miewe but backed out for various reasons and Miewe seems to have applied no pressure for them to continue. In one case the deal was called off because the slaughter room was too cold. Miewe later appealed against his manslaughter conviction on the grounds (as with his defence) that his victim was a willing participant.

Rehabilitation of the Wolf and Werewolf

Such evidence as we have, in the form of cave paintings and the like, suggests that the wolf was just one of many animal forms that a shaman might magically assume in ancient times, with no special horror attached to it. Therianthropy, or the idea that humans can either enter or take on the form of animals is as ancient as humans themselves.

As hunters, humans would naturally want to acquire or steal some of the wolf's prowess in the same field. The demonisation of the wolf and werewolf almost certainly began when humans settled to farming and when their livestock became sitting prey for the hungry wolf.

Every culture has its equivalent of the werewolf. In Africa there are leopard men, in South America jaguar men and so on. Wherever there are predators dangerous to humans there has traditionally existed the belief that some humans can either become or control them for their own purposes, and this remains a popular view in wide tracts of the world today.

In the modern West this has come to be considered mere superstition or delusion, apart from rare instances like those mentioned above. Also there has been a rehabilitation of the wolf now that it has become a negligible danger. In nature reserves it has come to be seen as a creature of beauty with admirable social skills and its contribution to the balance of life in the wild has come to be appreciated. The Kevin Costner film *Dances With Wolves* (1990) reflects this changing perspective.

This is almost a return to the probable original hunter-gatherer and Native American view of the wolf as an admirable and only occasionally to be feared rival.

It is increasingly recognised that the more recently traditional view of the wolf as a completely savage monster was a demonised projection. But this is so deeply embedded in the fairytales on which we are weaned that it is unlikely to melt away overnight. Madmen who become possessed of the notion that they have changed into wolves are still likely to shock the world occasionally with totally out of control savagery for a long while yet.

FURTHER READING

The Beast Within: A History of the Werewolf
Douglas, Adam. Avon Books, New York 1992

The Book of the Werewolf
Baring-Gould, Sabine. Studio Editions, London 1995
(facsimile of 1865 edition)
Online edition: www.unicorngarden.com/bov/sabine.htm

The Encyclopedia of Vampires, Werewolves, and Other Monsters
Guiley, Rosemary Ellen. Checkmark Books, London 2005

Vampires, Werewolves and Demons
Noll, Richard (Ed). Brunner/Mazel, New York 1992

The Werewolf: in Legend, Fact, and Art
Copper, Basil. St Martin's Press, London 1977

The Werewolf in Lore and Legend
Summers, Montague. Dover, New York 2003
(Facsimile of 1933 edition)

Online Sources

Encyclopedia Mythica
www.pantheon.org

Fortean Times
www.forteantimes.com

Werewolf Legends from Germany
Ed D. L. Ashliman, University of Pittsburgh
www.pitt.edu/~dash/werewolf.html

Wikipedia
www.wikipedia.com

Various

http://members.tripod.com/alam25
www.crystalinks.com/werewolves.html
www.wsu.edu/~delahoyd/werewolves.html
www.occultopedia.com
www.absoluteastronomy.com/encyclopedia/w/we/werewolf.htm